# The Bearskinner

A Story by the Brothers Grimm
with pictures by
Felix Hoffmann

A Margaret K. Mc Elderry Book
Atheneum . 1978 . New York

*For Katrin and Barbara*

Library of Congress catalog card number: 77-92742
ISBN 0-689-50123-4
Copyright © 1977 by Sauerländer AG, Aarau
Translation copyright © 1978 by Atheneum Publishers
All rights reserved
Printed and bound in Germany
First American Edition

Once there was a young man who wanted to be a soldier. He went off to war and fought bravely in the front line. But when the war was over, he was no longer needed, so he was discharged.

The soldier owned nothing but his rifle, which he put over his shoulder. Then he set off into the world to seek his fortune. Before long he came to a barren heath where nothing grew but a circle of trees. He

sat down beneath one of the trees. "I have no money," he thought sadly. "I have learned nothing but soldiering. Now that the war is over, I have no way to earn a living. I will starve if I don't find work."

All of a sudden, he heard a rustling in the trees, and an imposing-looking stranger in a long green coat stood before him. There was only one odd thing about the stranger—one of his feet was shaped like a horse's hoof.

"I know what you need," said the man. "Money and property. You shall have as much as you can ever use, but first I must know that nothing will frighten you. Otherwise, my money would be wasted."

"A soldier is never afraid," the soldier said. "Just try me!"

"Well," said the man, "look behind you!"

The soldier turned and saw a great bear coming toward him, growling fiercely. "Oho!" said the soldier, aiming his rifle. "I'll tickle your nose till you stop growling." He shot the bear, and the huge beast fell to the ground and never moved again.

"I can see that you have plenty of courage," said the stranger, "but there's one thing still you must agree to before I will make you rich."

"If it doesn't harm my soul," replied the soldier, who by now had guessed who the man was. "Otherwise, I won't agree."

"Listen and you'll see for yourself," the man replied. "For seven years, you are not to wash yourself or comb your beard and hair or cut your nails, and you must not pray. I will give you a coat and a cloak that you must wear during the seven years. If you die during that time, you will belong to me forever, but if you live you will be free and rich for the rest of your life."

The soldier thought how poor and hungry he was. "I've often faced death," he thought. "I can surely do this," and he agreed to the bargain.

The devil—for the stranger was none other—took off his green coat, gave it to the soldier, and said, "When you wear this coat and reach into the pocket, you will always find a handful of gold."

Then he skinned the bear and said, "This shall be your cloak and also your bed. You must sleep in it and in no other bed. And because of that cloak, you shall be called the Bearskinner." Then the devil vanished.

The soldier put on the coat, reached quickly into the pocket, and found a handful of gold coins, as the devil had promised. He put the bearskin around his shoulders and set off into the world in fine spirits.

For the first year he just looked like a man wearing a bearskin, but by the second year he looked like a monster.

His face was covered with hair, his beard was a tangled mess, his fingernails were like claws, and there was so much dirt on him that if someone had planted grass it would have sprouted. People ran away when they saw him, but since he gave money to the poor wherever he went, so that they would pray for him to stay alive during the seven years, and since he paid for everything he needed, he always found shelter.

In the fourth year he came to an inn where the innkeeper refused to give him a room. He would not even let him sleep in the stable, for fear he would frighten the horses. But when the Bearskinner reached into his pocket and pulled out a handful of gold pieces, the innkeeper relented. And when the Bearskinner promised to let no one see him, so that the inn's good reputation would not be harmed, the innkeeper took him in.

As the Bearskinner sat alone, wishing the seven years were up, he heard loud crying in the next room.

He was a kind man and he opened the door to see who was crying. He found an old man holding his head in his hands and sobbing bitterly. The Bearskinner came closer to comfort him, but the old man jumped up and tried to run away. When, however, he heard a human voice, he stopped in amazement, and after listening to the Bearskinner's story he told him his own troubles. Once he had had plenty of money, but it had all been spent, and now he and his daughters were starving. He was so poor that he couldn't even pay the innkeeper and would surely be sent to prison.

"If money is your only need," said the Bearskinner, "I can help you." He called for the innkeeper, paid the old man's bill, and slipped a bag full of gold pieces into his pocket.

"How can I thank you?" the old man said, when he saw that he was saved. "My daughters are beautiful. Come with me and choose one for your wife. When she hears what you have done for me, she won't refuse you. Though you look a little strange, she will soon change all that."

The Bearskinner liked the idea and followed the old man home. But when the eldest daughter saw him, she was so terrified by his looks that she screamed and ran away.

The second one took time to examine him from head to foot, but then she said, "How can I marry a man who hardly looks human? I once saw a real bear with his fur shaved off, wearing a soldier's uniform and white gloves and pretending to be a man. I quite liked him. This one is too hairy, besides being ugly. I can never marry him."

But the youngest daughter said, "Dear father, since this man helped you, he must be a good person. If you promised him a bride in exchange for his kindness, we must keep our word."

Beneath the hair and dirt that covered him, the Bearskinner's heart jumped for joy when he heard this. He took a ring from his finger, broke it in two, gave the girl one half and kept the other for himself. On her half, he wrote his name, on his he wrote her name, and he begged her to take good care of it.

Then sadly he said goodbye to her. "I must wander for three more years," he said. "If I don't come back to you, it means I have died and you will be free. Pray for me that I may live."

The poor bride dressed in black to show her sorrow, and when she thought of her bridegroom, tears filled her eyes. Her sisters only laughed at her.

"Be careful," said the eldest. "When you give him your hand, he'll scratch you with his claws."

"Watch out," said the second. "Bears love sweet things, and if he likes you he'll eat you up."

"You must always do what he tells you," continued the eldest. "Otherwise, he'll start growling."

The second chimed in, "But the wedding will be fun because bears dance so well."

The bride kept quiet and tried not to mind their teasing.

The Bearskinner roamed the world, from one place to another, doing good deeds where he could and giving money to the poor to pray for him. At last the day came when his seven years were up. He went to the barren heath and sat under the circle of trees.

Before long, he heard a whistling wind, and the devil stood before him looking very sour. He threw the old soldier's coat at the Bear-skinner.

"Not so fast," said the Bearskinner. "First you'll have to clean me up."

The devil didn't like that at all, but he had to fetch some water and wash the Bearskinner. He combed and trimmed his hair, shaved off his beard, and cut his nails.

The Bearskinner looked like a brave soldier again, more handsome than ever.

When the devil had gone, the Bearskinner's heart felt as light as a feather.

He went into the town and bought a beautiful velvet coat and a
carriage drawn by four white horses. Then he drove to his bride's

house. No one recognized him. The old man thought he was a colonel
in the cavalry, led him in, and introduced him to his two eldest

daughters. They poured wine for him, served him the choicest foods, and thought they had never seen a handsomer man. But the bride sat opposite him in her black dress, looking down and not saying a word.

When he finally asked the old man if he would give him one of his daughters as a wife, each of the two eldest thought she had been chosen. They ran to put on their finest dresses.

The Bearskinner, as soon as he was alone with his true bride, pulled out his half of the ring and threw it into a cup of wine which he handed to her. She took it and drank the wine. When she saw the ring in the bottom of the cup, her heart began to beat fast. She took the other half from a ribbon she wore around her neck, held the two pieces together and saw that they fitted each other perfectly.

"I am the man you met as a bearskinner," he said, "and I have come back to you looking like a man again." Then he took her in his arms and kissed her.

In the meantime, the two sisters had come back in their fanciest dresses. When they saw that the handsome stranger had chosen the youngest daughter and that he was the bearskinner they had refused three years before, they were so full of rage and venom that they

rushed out of the house and never came back.